SIMON &
SCHUSTER
BOOKS FOR
YOUNG READERS
An imprint of Simon &
Schuster Children's Publishing
Division ~ 1230 Avenue of
the Americas, New York, New York 10020

Book design
by Dan Potash ~ The text for this book is set in Iskoa and
National Primary. ~ The illustrations for this book are rendered in
colored pencils and watercolor. Manufactured in China

Library of Congress Cataloging-in-Publication Data ~ Goodrich, Carter.

~ A creature was stirring / by Clement C. Moore ; illustrated by Carter Goodrich.— 1st ed.

p. cm. ~ Summary: As a family lives out the famous poem by Clement Moore, a young boy

is unable to sleep and, in his excitement, performs several deeds bound to place him on the naughty

list, and one that just might save him. ~ ISBN-13: 978-0-689-86399-8

ISBN-10: 0-689-86399-3 ~ [1. Christmas—Fiction. 2. Santa Claus—Fiction. 3. Boys—Fiction.

4. Stories in rhyme.] I. Moore, Clement Clarke, 1779-1863. Night before Christmas. II. Title.

PZ8.3.G62495Cre 2006 ~ [E]—dc22 ~ 2006000343

2 4 6 8 10 9 7 5 3 1

first
edition

For Mom and Dad, with love—C. G.

A Creature Was Stirring

One Boy's Night Before Christmas

By Clement C. Moore and Carter Goodrich

Illustrated by Carter Goodrich

Simon & Schuster Books for Young Readers

New York   London   Toronto   Sydney

You all know this tale,
but read this, you'll see:
One creature was stirring,
that creature was me!

'Twas the night before Christmas, when all through the house
not a creature was stirring, not even a mouse.
The stockings were hung by the chimney with care,
in hopes that St. Nicholas soon would be there.

I don't want to butt in,
but I'm wide awake,
and in Santa's book
that's a naughty mistake.

The children were nestled all snug in their beds,
while visions of sugar plums danced in their heads.
And Mama in her kerchief, and I in my cap,
had just settled our brains for a long winter's nap.

How can they sleep?
I sure wish I could.
He'll write in that book;
he'll write I'm no good!

When out on the lawn there arose such a clatter,
I sprang from my bed to see what was the matter.
Away to the window I flew like a flash,
tore open the shutters, and threw up the sash.

He's here! I can hear him!
Now what do I do?
Don't panic, don't move . . .
look fast asleep too!

The moon on the breast of the new-fallen snow
gave the luster of midday to objects below,
when, what to my wondering eyes should appear,
but a miniature sleigh and eight tiny reindeer.

I might as well look
to be sure that he's real.
My friend says he's not,
but that's not how I feel.

With a little old driver, so lively and quick,
I knew in a moment it must be St. Nick.
More rapid than eagles his coursers they came,
and he whistled, and shouted, and called them by name.

My gosh, there he is!
And I'm in for it now.
I've been naughty twice.
To look's not allowed.

"Now, Dasher! Now, Dancer!
Now, Prancer and Vixen!
On, Comet! On, Cupid!
On, Donner and Blitzen!
To the top of the porch!
To the top of the wall!
Now dash away! Dash away!
Dash away all!"

They're coming up now!
They're moving this way!
St. Nicholas, toys,
reindeer, and sleigh!

As dry leaves that before the wild hurricane fly,
when they meet with an obstacle, mount to the sky,
so up to the house-top the coursers they flew,
with the sleigh full of toys, and St. Nicholas too.

Okay, try to calm down
and climb back in bed.
Don't look like you're breathing. . . .
Pretend that you're dead!

And then, in a twinkling, I heard on the roof
the prancing and pawing of each little hoof.
As I drew in my head, and was turning around,
down the chimney St. Nicholas came with a bound.

He's landed above!
His sleigh's just outside!
Wow, look at that thing.
Oh man, what a ride!

He was dressed all in fur, from his head to his foot,
And his clothes were all tarnished with ashes and soot.
A bundle of toys he had flung on his back,
and he looked like a peddler just opening his pack.

That sleigh is still moving.
If I'm not mistaken . . .
didn't he put
the sleigh parking brake on?

His eyes—how they twinkled! His dimples, how merry!
His cheeks were like roses, his nose like a cherry!
His droll little mouth was drawn up like a bow,
and the beard of his chin was as white as the snow.

Oh, what was that rhyme?
That command they all knew?
He shouted it once
and this thing really flew.

The stump of a pipe he held tight in his teeth,
and the smoke it encircled his head like a wreath.
He had a broad face and a little round belly,
that shook when he laughed, like a bowl full of jelly.

Come on, Dasher!
Go, Comet!
Do something, Cupid!
That's it, dash away!
(Gosh, I feel sorta stupid.)

He was chubby and plump, a right jolly old elf,
and I laughed when I saw him, in spite of myself.
A wink of his eye and a twist of his head
soon gave me to know I had nothing to dread.

Okay, easy does it.
Just put her down nice.
If he catches me now,
he writes "naughty"
thrice.

Quick! Back inside!
Now, reindeer, you
STAY!
That thing's safely parked.
Let's keep it that way.

He sprang to his sleigh, to his team gave a whistle,
and away they all flew like the down of a thistle.
But I heard him exclaim, 'ere he drove out of sight,

"HAPPY CHRISTMAS TO ALL,

and to all
a good night!"